BILLY BUDD
IN THE
BREADBOX

The Story of
Herman Melville and Eleanor

BY JANA LAIZ
Illustrations by Declan Kerr

Crow Flies Press ❀ South Egremont, MA

CROW FLIES PRESS
PO BOX 614 SOUTH EGREMONT, MA 01258 (413)-281-7015
www.crowfliespress.com
publisher@crowfliespress.com

Cover art and illustrations by Declan Kerr
Book design by Anna Myers

Billy Budd in the Breadbox
The Story of Herman Melville and Eleanor
Library of Congress Control Number: 2017954689
ISBN 978-0-9983139-1-7
Copyright © 2017 Crow Flies Press
Printed in the USA

ALSO BY JANA LAIZ

Elephants of the Tsunami

Weeping Under This Same Moon

The Twelfth Stone

Thomas & Autumn

"A Free Woman On God's Earth"
The True Story of
Elizabeth Mumbet Freeman,
The Slave Who Won Her Freedom

Simon Says; Tails Told By
The Red Lion Inn Ambassador

Blanket of Stars (coming soon)

DEDICATION

This book is dedicated to the memory of grandfathers, Nitong, Milton and Ben. I wish you were still here to share your stories.

To my dad, Poppa to my own children, whose love and support sustain me in more ways than I can say. I hope you will continue to share your special stories with us for a long time to come.

And for grandfathers and grandmothers everywhere. Talk to your grandchildren, tell them your stories, share your history and always keep true to the dreams of your youth.

PRAISE FOR BILLY BUDD IN THE BREADBOX

"Herman Melville comes to life in all his complex glory in this delightful story of a granddaughter's love for an old man whose last days are lived in obscurity but whose mind and heart are still full of life and genius. Jana Laiz's book is one that all readers touched by Melville's brilliance will treasure as a surprisingly intimate glimpse into the private world of one of America's greatest authors."

> Michael Shelden
> Author of *Melville in Love*

"*Billy Budd in the Breadbox* paints an enchanting portrait of Herman Melville and his granddaughter, capturing the special relationship between them. Based on a true story about a long-held secret and an amazing discovery, this captivating work of fiction will surprise and delight readers of all ages."

> Barbara Weisberg
> Author of *Susan B. Anthony, Woman Suffragist*

"Such a warm and thoughtful account of this tender relationship between my great-great aunt Eleanor and my great-great-great grandfather Herman Melville.

The manuscript becomes a magical object. It is first a secret between Melville and Eleanor, which then becomes the key to Melville's legacy. It reveals that writers live on through their work and can connect with the world long after their time on earth is through."

Elizabeth Doss, author of *Poor Herman*, Great-great-great granddaughter of Herman Melville

"Herman Melville was grandfather to my Great Aunt Eleanor and my grandmother Jeannette, who I named Granny Star for a star blouse she wore. Katherine was Aunt Kay. And Frances was always Aunt Tassie. I wonder if that wasn't a childhood nickname. After reading *Redburn*, I wish I had known him, but I was almost 50 years too late. I think Jana Laiz's book is wonderfully evocative of times gone by. The story of leaving the girls in the park was told me over and over as a child. And Jana has brought it to life. Un grand merci from my sister Betsy and me."

Allan Melville Chapin, great-great-great grandson of Herman Melville

"This wonderful book humanizes the great Herman Melville with humor, a terrific sense of history and a sweetheart of a young woman at its center named Eleanor!"

Kate Maguire
Artistic Director, CEO
Berkshire Theatre Group

"Jana Laiz employs the intuitions of childhood in her new biography of Herman Melville. She allows a true voyage of discovery to unfold the great writer's history and his secrets with the unparalleled enthusiasm of a young girl who loves unconditionally and employs her natural curiosity in the exploration of her forebear. The charms of youth and the caginess of age combine in this book to produce insights unforeseen. The title should provoke interest and the realization of young Eleanor's search for truth and surreptitious hints is captivating and energizing. For young readers, or their elders reading the book aloud, this should be a non-stop adventure into the life of an extraordinary man and his equally captivating grandchild."

J. Peter Bergman
Author of "*Small Ironies*"

"This heart-warming child's-eye view of Herman Melville gives us insight into the warmth and humor that made him one of our greatest American authors. Jana Laiz paints a vivid portrait of the love between young Eleanor and her illustrious grandfather, creating a page-turner of a historical novel that educates as much as it entertains."

Jennifer Browdy, Ph.D.
Author of *What I Forgot...And Why I Remembered*

CONTENTS

BILLY BUDD
IN THE
BREADBOX

The Story of
Herman Melville and Eleanor

NEW YORK CITY 1890

GRANDDAD HAS A SECRET

My grandfather has a secret. He keeps it in the folds of his black coat and tucked in that long gray beard of his that nearly hides his face. I see it in his eyes, this secret. It's there when we go for our walks through the streets of the city and when we sit down for supper. I spot it when we go to the park. I notice it when he doesn't know I am looking at him, especially then.

My sister doesn't see it. Not even the time he took her to the park and left her there by mistake. He was so far away that day, that he dropped her hand and simply walked away, leaving her all alone. She was only four at the time. She found her way home and I heard mother yelling at Granddad when he returned to the house. "How could you leave a child alone in Madison Square Park?" she had scolded him. He heard her, but I'm not sure he was really listening. I am determined to find out this secret of his. It makes him wistful and sad.

I often wonder if it has something to do with the books he writes. Wrote, I should say. He only writes poems now. But when he did write books, he wrote big, fat books that are difficult for me to read, and I'm a great reader. One day, I hope to read the books he has written. Mama tells me a nine-year-old girl wouldn't understand them yet. I'm sure she is right, and I would like to try, but Mama won't let me. I once asked Granddad if he would read one to me, the one about the whale. He laughed a bit and said, "Now why would you want to hear that? No one else did." And he walked away.

A student came to the house and asked to

see the great author, Herman Melville. When Granddad came out, the young man looked like he was going to faint and I saw his hand shaking a little as he held it out to Granddad. Later I asked Granddad if he was famous. He laughed very loudly but did not answer me.

On nights when I can't sleep I creep down to Granddad's study to see if he is also awake. When I don't find him at his desk, I imagine he is already asleep in his room, snoring in that dark bed of his, but some nights he is there, his face glowing eerily by candlelight. The other night I saw him scribbling with his quill. When he saw me, he quickly put his papers in the drawer and blew out the candle,

leaving me in the dark. I wonder what he is up to.

I am determined to read his books, and soon. Maybe they will reveal this secret of his. The best time I can get Granddad to talk is when we walk, so my legs are very strong, for I pull on his coat daily and make him take to the streets. Some days we walk past the big church, where Granddad never enters, past the post office, around the block, to the seaport, his favorite place. Some days I run or skip along ahead of him. Then he calls, "Look out, or the cop might catch you!" That makes me laugh. "Cop" is so much jollier a word than "policeman."

Sometimes we walk with no destination. Those are the days I like best. Today is a good day; Granddad is in a chatty mood.

"Eleanor, come sit down on this bench. I smell pines, do you smell them?" I do not, but I nod. I smell the damp salt air.

"I planted pines at Arrowhead. I watched them grow. I planted them when your mother was just a baby." He points upward. "These

masts remind me of them." Granddad points
to the tall masts of the ships.

"They stand on the south lawn, those ever-
greens. Oh, how your grandmother fumed
when she saw me planting useless pines on
the lawn instead of apple or pear. 'Useless!'
I said, 'have you never smelled the scent of
pine?' I suppose she had not, being from the
city, but I had spent my boyhood in Pittsfield
at my uncle's house and tramped through the
woods every day I was there. I love the scent
of pine." He breathes deeply and I watch his
nostrils flair.

"Breathe with me child." I do. He breathes
again and takes my hand in his. I close my eyes
and in my vision, I see tall pines with cones
hanging from them. The fragrance is strong
in my nostrils as I breathe deeply. When I
open my eyes, I am in New York again.

"Where's Pittsfield?" I ask, though I know
where it is. I want to hear Granddad talk
about that place. His eyes always shine a little
brighter when he speaks of it.

"In Berkshire. That's my heart's home.

The woods, the hills, the birdsong. Looking out my fairy window."

"What's a fairy window, Granddad?"

"Have you never looked out a fairy window, dear Tittery-Eye?"

He loves to call me by that silly name. I shake my head.

"It's a special portal that when you look through it at just the right angle, you see magic. The light comes through it just so and it can take you out of yourself and bring you around the world. In my study, looking out that window, I found myself on many shores."

"Is that not your imagination?" I know about that. I imagine many things.

"I suppose you might say that, and I am sure if one were to close one's eyes and look inward one might see the things I saw, but it's so pleasant looking out over the hills and meadows through the wavy glass and suddenly finding oneself on the rolling ocean aboard a sailing ship or tramping through an ancient forest."

"Is there a fairy window on 26th street that

I could look out of, Granddad?"

"None that I have found, but you can go through the house and look out all the windows, and there are many, and see what you can see."

"I think I will."

"You do that."

He looks wistful again and I wonder if I did right by speaking of it. But he brightens and says, "One day, dear Eleanor, I will bring you there and I will let you look out my window." He pats me on the head though I know he never will. Pittsfield is far away from

New York City, all the way in Massachusetts and Granddad is an old man.

But he wasn't always old and before he leaves us for his heavenly home, which I am fearful will be soon, I am determined to know about him. I am a very inquisitive girl, or so my mother says all the time. Too inquisitive. But how can anyone be too curious? Doesn't everyone want to know everything one can?

My grandfather is a storyteller and if I'm too young to read his stories, like Mama says, then I want to hear his stories, straight from the man himself.

HERMAN MELVILLE,
MY GRANDDAD

The days we visit Granddad Herman and Grandmamma Lizzie are my very favorites. My friends in New Jersey cannot understand why this is so, and once, I even brought my friend Sophie with me to meet my grandfather. She was terrified of him and hardly spoke to me for days after that visit. She thought his beard too long and his eyes too dark, and him too gruff. That made me sad, but not sad enough to think too much about it. I will not invite her back to 26th street. I will keep Granddad to myself.

I know I should spend more time with Grandmamma Lizzie than I do, but she is not as interesting as Granddad. His imagination is full and when he is in a mood, he tells me stories. Grandmamma only cooks and makes things out of wool and lace. Sometimes I wish I were a boy so I could do more adventurous things, like my grandfather did when he was young. Whenever I ask Mama if I can do something exciting, like climb the elm tree near our house or ride a bicycle, she says no.

I never tell Mama that days at Granddad's are so much more interesting than staying home in Orange. Our house in New Jersey is nowhere near as interesting as Granddad's. There are all sorts of curious rooms in the house on 26th street. If I told her, she might make me stay at home.

"Come Eleanor, just look at those hills." Granddad takes my hand, and points upward. From the window of his study I see buildings, but that is not what he sees. He sees the mountains he loves. If I looked into his eyes, I might see the mountain reflected there, the one he calls Charlemagne. The one that inspired him.

"Granddad, who is Charlemagne?"

"Charlemagne was a king a long time ago. A very wise king."

"Is that why you named your mountain Charlemagne?"

"Smart girl. My mountain is the king of mountains; indeed, it is."

Mama tells me that when he was writing *Moby-Dick*, that book about the whale, Granddad locked himself in his study and no amount of pounding on the door would make him leave until he was ready.

"Your Aunt Bessie and I knocked and knocked, but he wouldn't come out until he was ready. Your uncle Stanwix sometimes lay on the floor, looking under the door to see what went on in that study. 'Feet's all I can see' he would say," Mama tells me.

"Maybe he didn't want to be interrupted. Sometimes I don't want to be."

Mama gives me a long look. "You're right about that, but we might have liked to play with him. We thought he might want a rest."

His eyes are bad from a sickness he had when he was little, and they are worse still from all that writing by candle and dim light. At Arrowhead, they did not have gas lamps, like we do now in the city. Just the light coming in from the windows.

Granddad wrote facing the north side, the side facing his mountain, so it must have been fairly dark in the afternoon and cold and gray on a winter's day. Brrrr, it makes me shiver to even think about it.

Mama says that her Aunt Augusta, Granddad's sister, was the only one allowed into his study. She went there every day after he stopped writing, to rewrite Granddad's scribble in her own fine hand, so that in the morning, Granddad could clearly read what he had written the day before.

"But Aunt Augusta was never, ever allowed to put in any punctuation! Papa wanted to add that himself."

I wonder how he could understand what he had written with no commas or periods.

"Granddad, why did you not let my great-aunt Augusta put punctuation marks on your writing?" I urge.

"For what reason under the sun do you want to know that?!"

"I might want to be a great writer like you one day, so I must know all about you." Granddad looks at me with amusement.

"But you are a writer," he says with all seriousness.

"What do you mean?"

"See here," he says, pulling a parchment out of his desk, "I have a letter from a very excellent four-year-old writer."

Granddad unfolds the paper and reads: "My dear Grandpa, Frances and I have got a new doll, my dolly's name is Dinah and Frances' dolly's name is Susie and you haven't seen them. When I was getting into bed, I saw a 'ittle fly in the water…"

I put my hands over my eyes! "Did I really write "'ittle'?"

"You did. Shall I continue?"

"No Granddad, please tell me about *you*!"

"The letter ends very well, though. 'We had 'ittle tiny kitties and they have runned away. I send a kiss to Grandpa. From Eleanor M. Thomas.' You see? A writer, like your old grandpa. Here's a kiss back." And he kisses me on the cheek. It tickles.

He slowly folds the parchment and places it in his drawer. It makes me feel full that he has saved that letter from when I was so young.

"Granddad, but you didn't answer me."

"You are a persistent little bug, aren't you? To my way of thinking, punctuation makes the written word come to life. You can change the entire meaning by an omission or misplacement of even a comma. So, I would not allow my sister to do that, lest she make a mistake when transcribing my writing."

"I think you're right, Granddad. I will not let anyone punctuate my writing either when I'm a writer. Can you write a story with me and Frances as your characters?"

He frowns. Frances comes running into the room and throws herself onto Granddad. "Make a story 'bout me, Grandda," she says. I wonder if she was listening at the door. Sometimes it is annoying having a little sister, but other times it is all right. Just last week, I tied her to the bedpost and pretended she was my prisoner. When Mama called us down for supper, I ran down and forgot about untying her until Papa, Mama and I sat at the table.

"Wherever is Frances?" Mama had asked. Suddenly I remembered.

"Oh, I'll get her!" and I ran upstairs before anyone could say another word. She never even told on me. She believed she was a naughty prisoner and didn't move until I let her go.

Granddad bounces Frances on his knee. I climb on the other one and he grasps each of us, bouncing us a few times, then puts us down on the floor. Frances runs out again, as fast as she entered.

There is still so much I want to know about him. I know if I can make him talk, he might reveal his secret to me, so I smile up at him, pulling on his sleeve.

"Granddad, tell me about when you were my age," I urge. Some days he will talk.

"Let's sit outside on the bench and I will tell you a bit, until you yawn with boredom."

"But I won't yawn," I say with all serious-ness. We walk out of the front door and sit on the bench just outside the house. I snuggle beside him.

He pats me on the head, leans back and sighs deeply.

"Did you know I had to leave school when I was only twelve?"

I shake my head.

"Yes, my father was a terrible business man and when I was only a lad of eleven, he went bankrupt. Do you know what that means?"

I shake my head again.

"He lost all our money, every penny. So, he pulled me out of school, which I was none too keen about since I liked learning and was a good student, and he dragged my brothers, sisters, mother and me away from the city and all the way to Albany, New York to live with my grandmother, who was none too pleased to have us."

"If my father went bank up..."

"Bankrupt," Granddad corrects.

"Bankrupt, you would have me and Frances, wouldn't you?"

"Of course, of course."

"Did you ever go back to school, Granddad?"

"I took to the sea." He says and looks wistful again. Is that where his secret hides? I tug on his arm and he shakes himself and returns to me.

"But that was later. To answer your question, yes, I did go back to school for a brief time." Granddad shakes his head. "We had lived a grand life before Albany, child, right here in this great metropolis. Grander than you can imagine. Our parlor was filled with beauty. Paintings from France, rare objects of great value, books of Rousseau, Voltaire, Racine! Oh, how I loved the feel of those leather books in my hands. My father was elegance itself; we even had a family crest. And he was the perfect example, if ever there was one, of aristocracy ~ incapable of maintaining himself or his family. Completely impractical! And as for business, well, he was a great borrower. Always in debt, always scheming for ways to make money. We children never knew how bad it was, until the day we lost everything. My own grandfather, your great-great-grandfather turned away from his own son, so ashamed was he. But I loved my father.

"One day, the world crashed down upon us, and we had to escape like thieves in the night."

I hold my breath, not wanting to say

anything to interrupt this current. Granddad closes his eyes for a moment, remembering. The sun disappears behind a cloud. I shiver a little, but say not a word. I am secretly praying he will continue. I let my breath out ever so softly, not wanting even to remind him I am here.

"It was a chilly October. My older brother Gansevoort had escorted my mother, your great-grandmother, Maria, and my brothers and sisters to Albany, to live with my mother's family. They had taken what they could carry of our possessions. My father and I were alone in the house, packing up the rest of our belongings. It was rather eerie with my mother and my seven brothers and sisters gone. The furniture was left behind for my father and me to bring up the Hudson River, like bandits. The creditors were chasing my father to pay his debts. We had little choice but to run. You know, if my father had been caught, it would have been debtor's prison for sure."

"What's that? Would they have *shackled*

him?" I imagine my great-grandfather in chains of iron.

"Not necessarily, but my father would have had to work to pay off his debts, and for him, that might have been worse than shackles. And we would have been plunged into poverty. Not that my grandmother was generous, she was not. But we at least had a roof over our heads and food to eat.

"And so, under the cover of darkness, my disgraced father and I left our grand home and traveled up the Hudson River to avoid the creditors who were after him. That was a cold night, but not the coldest I have ever spent. I was glad my father had asked me to stay behind to help. Even if it meant freezing myself on a flat barge floating up the Hudson River in the dead of night. It was bound to be an adventure and I loved adventure and I think," he pauses, his eyes sparkling for a brief moment, "my father did as well."

"Did you miss your home?"

"Certainly, I did. I remember the feelings swelling inside me, as the wagon jerked to a

start. I had tried to keep my composure but it was hard not to be afraid and nostalgic. But my father had placed his arm around my shoulders and pulled me next to him. This show of affection was rare and I relished my time with him." Granddad pauses for a moment looking into his memory. He pats his lap for me to climb on. I do and he hugs me tightly. I put my fingers into his bushy beard. He kisses me on the top of my head. I wonder if he is thinking about his father. I'm sure he is and it makes me love him even more.

"Our poor horse had to watch her step in the gloom until we got to the Hudson River dock and the barge we would board. I had been on ferries before, but never on such a large vessel. And never in the middle of the night. I led the mare onto the creaky platform and gave the poor old gal a bit of the carrot I had in my pocket. She was glad to have it. I snuggled next to her, her over-heated body keeping me warm. I saw my father breathe a huge sigh of relief as the city disappeared into the dark. The creditors would not find us."

I imagine my granddad as a boy just a little older than I am now. I close my eyes for just a moment and it is me on that barge. The air is cold and I snuggle into the horse's warmth. I open my eyes and I am once again sitting with my grandfather on the bench.

Even though I like it here in New York City better than Orange, I would be sad to leave my home and my room and my things.

I hug Granddad even more tightly. He hugs me again.

"We tried to keep up appearances in Albany. As I told you, my brothers, Gansevoort, Allan Jr., and I were even enrolled at the prestigious Albany Academy. No one knew of our disgrace, but it was difficult to be surrounded by boys of wealth and circumstance, knowing we would be amongst them as fellows had our father been more responsible with our fortune. I achieved high honors, the highest in arithmetic, I'll have you know and I was awarded first prize in my class. The principal, Mr. Beck, wrote an inscription to me. Let me think. Yes, 'the first best in class for ciphering books.' Ha! You did not know your Granddad was such a scholar."

"But of course I did!"

"Well, I'm glad of that. My father knew it too, briefly, dying the next year, leaving my poor mother a penniless widow with eight hungry children. Sounds rather dramatic, does it not?"

I nod my head.

"Poor Gansevoort. My older brother was sixteen at the time and schooling ended for him that day. I suppose mine did too. He left school and went to work in the fur trade. I left school a few months later as well, and accepted a job as a clerk in a bank that my mother's brother, my Uncle Peter obtained for me. I held that job for three years. I worked all the days of the week save Sunday and more hours than a child ought." Granddad looks sad again and I am afraid he will never say another thing to me.

"Ah, but I must not think on that time. You know, child, I wrote about that time in *Redburn*. Run into my study and get it off the shelf, if you would." I hop down off his lap and run inside to his study bookshelf to look for it. I wonder if he enjoys seeing his name on books. I know I would if ever I wrote one. I see many books, some with his name on them, others that say Hawthorne and many by Shakespeare. I see it there on a low shelf. The cover is dark blue cloth and the letters are gold. It says: *Redburn. Melville. New York.*

As I walk past Granddad's desk I think quickly about peeking around. I wonder if I might find his secret there amongst his things. But that would be deceitful, so I keep walking.

I bring the book out to him, and sit back on the bench beside him.

"Let me see." He shuffles the pages until he finds what he is looking for. "Here, child, read this passage here," he points.

I notice that his hand is shaking a little as I take the book from him. My heart feels strange to see that, but he wants me to read, and so I do.

"'*I must not think of the delightful days, before my father became bankrupt and died, and we removed from the city; for when I think of those days, something rises up in my throat and almost strangles me.*' Oh, Granddad!" This makes me feel sad.

"As I said, quite dramatic."

I pat Granddad's quivery hand. He takes mine and we intertwine our fingers.

Granddad pats my head.

"It reminds me of my nineteen exhausting years at the Customs House. Working all the days of the week save Sunday, earning four dollars a day. Ah, me. Makes me tired. Off you go, child, into the house. It is time for my nap."

I am disappointed, but Granddad needs to rest. I wish I could stay with him all day, for tomorrow we must return to New Jersey.

AUNT BESSIE LIVES HERE TOO

"**F**ather, enough gabbing. Come and take your rest." Aunt Bessie gives me an admonishing look. But then she winks. Granddad has been telling me about a time he and Grandmamma had gone over to London on a big boat, but he keeps nodding off, so I am not too upset that she has come in. She takes Granddad's hand in her twisted one and helps him to his room. I imagine they hurt, her hands. She's got something called arthritis, which causes terrible pain quite badly in both of them, but she still is ever so jolly.

I hope I never get arthritis. I might not

ever smile if I did. Once I fell and took the skin off my knee so badly that I had to cover it with a bandage for a week. Every time my mother changed the bandage I cried. I tried to be brave, but I was not. Not like Aunt Bessie.

Aunt Bessie lives here with Granddad and Grandmamma even though she is grown. Aunt Bessie never married. She helps her old parents and I wonder if she is the favorite child. I believe my mother thinks so. I wonder if it makes her jealous. But Mama only says good things about her big sister. She says she is brilliant and kind, and we must mind her. I am sure she feels sorry for her sister's painful affliction. I do think she is a bit envious though.

I might be jealous of my own little sister, but I'm too interested in other things to be jealous of her. She is very small and always leaving her toys about. Well, a few times perhaps I was jealous when Mama did not allow me to visit Granddad, but took only Frances. Mama said I was too headstrong and would upset my grandparents, and sweet little Frances would not. I'm sure Granddad missed my company on those horrid occasions for I do believe I am Granddad's favorite. I hope I am. He is mine. Although I have no other that I have ever met.

What I am happy about is that Mama lets us stay here on 26th Street quite often. New Jersey, where we live, is not too far away by train and ferry but I wish I lived in Manhattan. It's so much more exciting than silly old Orange. I must admit, though, I don't prefer the back parlor. I always run past the portraits that hang there. The eyes always seem to follow me, especially the portrait of Granddad made by Mr. Eaton. And poor Frances is terrified of Granddad's plaster busts, especially that of Antinous. She swears his head turns ever so slightly as she passes. I shiver to think on it.

We stay upstairs on the third floor in Mama's old room, right next door to Aunt Bessie.

Aunt Bessie taught herself to speak French and now she is teaching me. *Je parle français, et vous?* Aunt Bessie says the words and I repeat them. One – *un*, two – *deux*, three – *trois*... I can count to 100 and say things like "How do you do? *Comment allez-vous?*" and "Do you take milk or lemon with your tea? *Prenez-vous du lait ou citron avec votre thé?*" Granddad says that it is important to learn another language and that French is as good as any.

Some call Aunt Bessie "Old Maid" and spinster, but I think that is cruel. Maybe she never wanted to marry anyone. I'm sure I will never marry. I want to go to sea, like Granddad and visit places I have only seen on the pages of Granddad's large atlas. Some nights when I cannot sleep, I imagine myself a sea captain, standing on the deck with my hands behind my back, inspecting my sailors. The sails are billowing in the wind and my hair is whipping around my face. I am the only girl sea captain in the world, but I know more about sailing than any man, because my granddad taught me.

"Aunt Bessie, have you read any of Granddad's stories?"

"Of course. Why do you ask?"

"Mama won't let me read them. She says I am too young. How old were you when you read them?"

"I was already a grownup. I wasn't much interested in them when I was a child. I'm not as curious as you, dear Eleanor." Aunt Bessie kisses me on the top of my head.

"Well, I want to read them. So I can know all about Granddad."

"I will lend you one of mine, if you promise not to tell my sister." She winks at me and leaves the room.

Now that Granddad is napping I will spend some time in Grandmamma's room. Her bedroom is on the second floor and it is sunny and comfortable with a sewing machine and a white bed, like other people's. Granddad's room is much more somber and his bed is large and black. We are not allowed there, unless Granddad invites us. Maybe that is where he keeps his secret. A passageway connects their rooms and sometimes Granddad comes in and tells us stories.

"Grandmamma Lizzie, do you ever write stories like Granddad?"

She laughs. "No, I leave the writing to your grandfather. I prefer knitting. Would you like me to show you what I've been working on?"

Grandmamma Lizzie has a sewing and knitting box that is also a game table, where

Aunt Bessie and I sometimes play checkers. Mama tells me that when she was a little girl in Pittsfield, she used to play with her brothers and her sister on this very table. I love that it has two jobs. My grandmother pulls something soft looking and white out of the box.

"Feel this, dear."

It is soft as a lamb and very fine.

"What will it be, Grandmamma?"

"I think it will be a shawl. What do you think?"

"I think a shawl would be wonderful. It will be very elegant."

She laughs again and holds it up to me. "Hmmn, I think a few more inches and it might be just right for an elegant New Jersey girl, for when she takes strolls around the park with her handsome grandfather. Do you not agree?"

"Oh! Grandmamma, I love it!"

"It was going to be for your next birthday, but it's getting a bit cool, and I can't wait!"

I throw my arms around her. Just then, Granddad comes in from his nap.

"What's all this hugging about? Do I not get one too?"

I run into his arms and hug him tightly.

He lifts me up for a moment and I wonder that he is still strong. "Are you ready to come and let us see if our little butterfly has flown away?"

"Yes! Let's see," I say.

"Yes, Grandda!" yells my sister.

"Wait a moment, young ladies. You need your bonnets." Aunt Bessie brings Frances

and me our bonnets and ties the ribbons under our chins, even with her painful hands. I hope I will be as good as she when I am old.

Granddad, Frances and I walk downstairs to the little porch where Granddad's little red china butterfly match holder is still there, hanging on the wall. Granddad says we must check it daily to see if it has flown away.

"Hasn't flown yet. Maybe tomorrow." Granddad winks at us. I wink back. Frances tries to at least.

THERE ARE FAIRIES HERE

I t's been more than a month since I was
here on 26th Street and I am breathless as
I read what my own grandfather has written.
I plucked the book off the shelf in the parlor
at home when no one was looking, and am
happy that my mother did not find it in my
overnight case. I feel conspiratory, now I
have a secret too. But Granddad doesn't
know I know about his. I'm tempted to ask
him. We are in New York visiting Granddad
and Grandmamma. I'm sure there is a copy
of his *Piazza Tales* here, but I was enjoying it
at home and was afraid he would listen to his

daughter, my mother, and not allow me to read it. She only wants me to read things like *Glorious Times* or *Aesop's Fables* or my school primer. So, I put it deep inside my bag.

Here is my favorite passage of that story:

My horse hitched low his head. Red apples rolled before him — Eve's apples, seek-no-furthers. He tasted one, I another; it tasted of the ground. Fairyland not yet, thought I, flinging my bridle to a humped old tree, that crooked out an arm

to catch it. For the way now lay where path was none, and none might go but by himself, and only go by daring. Through blackberry brakes that tried to pluck me back, though I but strained toward fruitless growths of mountain laurel, up slippery steeps to barren heights, where stood none to welcome. Fairyland not yet, thought I, though the morning is here before me. Some haunted ring where fairies dance...

I feel caught in a green wonderland when I read that. Fairies and horses and apples. I can smell the wood smoke and the fresh air. I imagine myself dancing with fairies, their dresses and mine, all lacy and sparkly. I wonder why my mother said I would not understand what he writes. I do. What I cannot imagine is that my grandfather believes in fairies. I know I do, but I never guessed that the old man would too.

"I see a light under that door!" Granddad is coming to check on us. "What mischief is going on in there?"

"No mischief, Granddad!" I call and put the book under the covers.

Frances is sleeping and Granddad comes in quietly.

"What are you hiding, Tittery-Eye?" How does he know?

"I fear some mischief is occurring here, else why are you not asleep like the little one there?" he points to my sister.

"I was just reading a book."

"A book? What book? I see no book."

"If I tell you, will you promise not to tell Mama?"

"I knew there was some monkey business going on! Are you reading Mr. Poe? No, then you would be terrified. You do not look like you've seen a ghost. Who are you reading?"

"I'm reading Mr. Melville," I say teasingly.

Granddad sits on the end of my bed. "Ah, Mr. Melville. And what prose of Mr. Melville's would you be reading at this late hour?"

I pull the book from under the covers and show him.

"And which story?"

"*The Piazza*. Granddad, do you believe in faeries?"

"Of course."

"Have you ever seen one?"

"Many."

"Did they put a spell on you?"

"Of course. How do you think I became a mad writer?"

"Are they beautiful?"

"I had better say yes else they will put a wicked spell on me. Yes, yes, they are beautiful. Have you never seen one in New Jersey?"

"Are there fairies in New Jersey?"

"Why, there are fairies everywhere if one knows where to look."

"Are they here? In this house?"

"I haven't seen one in quite some time, but I'd say there is some likelihood. There might be one under your bed, or there, in your bureau."

I think he is teasing.

"Maybe there is one hiding in your beard!" I say and reach into that fuzzy thicket and pull.

"Ouch! I daresay, if one is hiding there, one would never find it. Now, it is late and time for little fairies, and girls for that matter, to enter dreamland."

I snuggle down under the quilt. Granddad kisses my head, and turns out the light. I watch him as he slowly walks out of the room. He turns once more in the dark and blows me a kiss.

GRANDDAD HERMAN AT
UNCLE THOMAS' HOUSE

G randdad is telling me about when he was a boy. He puts on different voices and it's almost as if I can hear my great-grandmother Maria yelling, "Herman, come down from that tree! Melvilles do not climb trees."

He puts on his own voice and says, "Oh yes they do, I said to myself. I was only thirteen at the time, but I had looked around from my perch high on the branch of the Oak at the edge of my uncle's field and was determined to stay up there. The Berkshire hills were shining with the colors of summer and I remember smelling the intoxicating fragrance of meadow sage and catmint. No, I did not want to come down."

"But did you? Did you come down? I want to climb a tree!"

"One day, my dear, you shall. And of course, I did, good son that I was, and I wondered how it was that my mother always caught me doing things like this. Like your mother, my headstrong daughter likely catches you," he winks at me. "She probably longed to do them herself. Being grown up must be unpleasant, I had mused. And I promised myself that I would never forget the feeling of the wind from up there. I would remember how it felt to climb high and breathe hard, no matter my age."

"And did you?"

"Of course I did. I still do. It's not something one forgets."

"But you're so old!" I say, then clap a hand over my mouth, but Granddad only laughs.

"My mother had stood there, tapping her foot impatiently. I shimmied down the tree, ripping my good breeches on my way down. I smiled when I saw what I had done." His eyebrows go up as he looks at me.

"I was a country boy; no matter I was raised in the city. To me, this was better than any city block in Manhattan or Albany. I wished we could stay forever."

"Did you stay for a while? You're a city man now, Granddad."

"I am, but the country is my first love. It was the first time I had been in Pittsfield, but it would not be the last. It was love at first sight! Being in those green and rolling hills gave me a feeling inside unlike any other. And staying at Uncle Thomas' house with so many cousins was heaven. Even your city-bred great-grandmother found country life charming. 'Breathe in the sweets, my children!' she said to us, sweeping the clean air with her arm and smiling for the first time since my father died earlier that year. And no, I did not stay forever," Granddad frowns, "but had to return to Albany where I worked at a bank."

"Oh, Granddad, I'm sorry you had to work. I might like to work when I am thirteen."

"No my dear, you would not. You will not. You will go to school and learn your letters and arithmetic and whatever it is you young people learn these days."

"But I might like to have money of my own."

Granddad tells me that the money he made went straight to his mother.

"I kept not a penny. Not even when your great-uncle Gansevoort and I raked and turned hay with Uncle Thomas and he gave us each a coin. Gave it right to my mother. I didn't mind, though, I loved the smell of the newly cut hay. I loved the swish of it as the sickle sliced it down." Granddad makes a swishing sound.

"'Smell the hay, boys! You'll not get a scent like this in the city, I can tell you!' Uncle Thomas said to us, and he was right. After all that hard work, we earned the penny and a swim. We stripped off our clothes and dove right into the Melville pond."

"Granddad!"

He laughs, "Don't be so shocked. There were no girls for miles, just my brother, boy cousins and me. And oh, could I swim. Like a fish under the cool, sweet water."

"Did you open your eyes under the water?

What did you see?"

"I did open my eyes and in that pond I saw fish and frogs, but I dreaded seeing snapping turtles, I can tell you!

"And then, to my vast disappointment, a letter came from my Uncle Peter in Albany. I was needed at the bank and must return. I was not to stay the summer, like the rest of the family. They needed me to run their errands for them."

"Did you cry? I would have cried," I say and pat the old man's hand. I pull my own tears back inside.

"I ran out of the house, letting the door slam behind me. I ran to the Oak and scrambled up that tree, sitting for a long time looking out at the hills, wiping away escaped tears. Climbing trees and rambling in the woods was much more interesting and I would have been happy to remain squirrel-like up in the Oak, looking out at the Berkshire Hills."

"Why could you not work for your Uncle Thomas instead?"

"I thought the same, and even asked my mother, but that request was met with a resounding no. I think she felt guilty but that did not stop her from putting me on the coach back to Albany the next day."

"I would have said to my mother, 'I would prefer not to,'" I add.

Granddad opens his eyes wide. "Eleanor Melville Thomas, have you been reading more of my stories?"

"Only when you are napping, like you said I could. I loved *Bartleby the Scrivener*! I want to say 'I would prefer not to' quite a lot. Especially when Mama says I must play with Frances."

"What secrets are you keeping from your mother?"

"Only a few. Not as many as you are hiding."

I clap my hand over my mouth, not really believing that I said it.

Granddad's eyebrows go up in that way of his.

"Perhaps you need to write a detective

story about a New Jersey girl and her insatiable curiosity. She solves mysteries. How would you like that?"

"I would rather you wrote one about me, Granddad. That I would like very much, and you can add Frances too, if you must."

"Me? I'm no longer allowed to write, don't you know!"

"I see you writing sometimes in your study," I say, feeling I am getting closer to his secret.

"You do, do you? Do not tell Winnie!"

"Who is Winnie? And why should I not tell her?"

Granddad laughs. "That is your grandmother. One of the pet names I call her. Winnefred."

"But why?"

"I call her Winnie after the Red clover we both love so well."

"No, Granddad, *why* should I not tell her you've been writing?" Granddad confuses me sometimes.

"You had better ask her."

"But, Granddad, if I ask her, won't she guess that you have?"

"Perhaps, but still, you may ask your grandmother why she forbids me to write. You may tell me her answer. No answer she has yet given me seems satisfactory. Perhaps you'll get the truth out of her."

I think I am a little bit closer to his secret.

The Berkshire Hills
For A Visit

"Look, Granddad, snow!" I see the flakes falling from the window in Granddad's study. "Shall we go out and catch the flakes on our tongues?"

"Your old grandfather is feeling rather creaky in the joints today. But I will watch you from the window if you want to play outside with Jack Frost."

I don't want to leave Granddad alone in the study. He might get lonesome. I see a woolen blanket hung over a chair and I bring it to him and put it around his shoulders. I kiss him on the cheek, his beard tickles my face. It is very cold today and ice crystals are forming on the window. But the fire in the hearth is crackling merrily.

"Tell me more about Berkshire, Granddad!"

"That I can do, easily and happily. Tea first, if you please."

I leave him sitting and go into the kitchen and ask Grandmamma Lizzie to make tea. The kitchen is cozy and warm and as I sit waiting for the water to boil I ask, "Grandmamma, why do you forbid Granddad to write anymore?"

She stops preparing the tea. She has her back to me, and she doesn't turn around as she answers. "The critics. They are so hard on him. He's not been the success he dreamed he'd be. We dreamed. I don't want any more pain for him." She turns around, wiping her hands on her apron as the water boils and sputters. "Oh dear," she says lifting the heavy teapot from the stove and pouring the water into the pretty china teapot. "Tea for two?"

"Yes, please, Grandmamma." I feel sad for her and Granddad. Their dreams did not come true. Is that why Granddad sometimes looks sad?

"You be careful, dear," she says, handing me the tea tray. She puts a small plate of figs on the tray.

"My Herman loves figs," she smiles. I can see that Grandmamma loves Granddad.

I carefully carry the heavy tea tray into his study and set it down. Granddad sees the figs and smiles. First he bites into one, and makes funny faces, rolling his eyes in apparent delight. I'm glad some things still make him happy. He then takes a slow sip of the tea.

"Now, where were we? Oh, I should think right now, my mountain, Charlemagne is resplendent white. Elegantly covered in the most expensive Chinese silk. The snow is deep, a foot, I daresay, or more. My window-panes are covered with a delicate frost that one might say was etched upon them. Or perhaps the faeries danced on the outside and left their tiny footprints. Is that better?"

"Oh yes, I like that."

"I knew you would. On a cold day like this, and there was many a cold day in Pittsfield, the fire would be blazing in my big chimney. Oh, you would have liked that chimney, Eleanor. It is the grandest hearth I know. I wrote an ode to that dear smoke-stack. My brother Allan had my words painted right into the stone and the panels above. He did that for your grandmother and my silver anniversary. 'I and my chimney, two grey-headed old smokers' it reads." My granddad laughs heartily. It is such an excellent sound.

"After my father's death, my mother brought us to my dear Uncle Thomas' house in Pittsfield. The cholera was moving near to Albany and my mother took us all to escape it. I sometimes thank God for that epidemic, for had it not come to town, my mother might never have taken us to Berkshire and I might never have discovered Arrowhead. And oh, the times we had at Uncle Thomas'! Cousins upon cousins! It was raucous and highly entertaining.

"I loved it there. I rambled the hills and tasted wild berries and I climbed trees. I crawled in caves. Can you imagine your old granddad like a bear in cave? Can you? I promise it is true. I loved the wildness and freedom. I wonder if you will remain a city girl or if you will be a country child, like I was. I was a farmer, you know."

"You were, never."

"There you are wrong. In this long life, I have been student, school teacher, farmer, sailor, whaler, customs officer, and some say writer."

"I know you were a writer, Granddad. I know that."

"How did you know? Who told you? Did your mother tell you? Did she tell you how she banged upon my study door to get me to stop writing and come down for supper?"

"She did, Granddad. She told me that some nights they brought your dinner up on a tray and left it by the door for you, like a prisoner. Why did you not want to eat in the dining room? Sometimes I do not want to eat in the dining room. Can I ask my mother to bring me dinner on a tray?"

My granddad laughs from his belly. "You may not, child. You are not so eccentric as your old granddad. Perhaps when you are old, you can ask your children to bring you your supper on a tray and leave it on the floor. Until then, you shall continue to be a civilized young lady."

I look disappointed and my granddad laughs again.

"Some nights, I wished to write long after the sun went down. My fairy window faced north, toward Charlemagne ~ Mt. Greylock and there were times, I was loath to leave my study, even for a bite to eat, though the darkness descended fast. These old eyes are tired from writing by candlelight.

"And I rose early, by eight and went to my barn. Most mornings I left your grandmother a-snoring. I always said good morning to Charlie, my horse, and then paid a visit to my cow. Did you know I had a cow?"

"I wish we had a cow."

"A cow on 26th Street, hmm, what would the neighbors say?"

"They might like fresh milk, Granddad!"

"They might indeed. But our milkman would be none too pleased, I should think."

"Did you milk the cow?"

"Of course I did, I loved milking. In fact, I most loved this quiet time in the barn. Just the sound of my cow's soft breathing and the zippy sound of milk hitting tin. Zing! Zing! This time gave me the uninterrupted quiet to prepare for my writing day. Many a thought formed and gathered in that barn. I would tuck them away where my other duties could not touch them, and I would bring them out later with my quill."

"Wasn't it cold in the barn?"

"On a winter's day, but cows care nothing for seasons. They need to be milked and fed all through the year. After milking, I fed my good cow pumpkin, too! Ah, she loved mashing that sweet soft pumpkin and chewing it like cud. And I loved standing by to watch her eat it. What a pleasant sight, seeing her jaws move so mildly and with such a sanctity." Granddad is lost in thought again, but he looks so content, that I drink my tea and let him savor for a few moments.

"I would say, 'And here is my good cow. I must think of a name for you. Giver of Milk seems too highfalutin, Blossom, too ordinary. You love your pumpkin, perhaps that name suits. Hmmn? Do you like Pumpkin? I will ask the children what they think. In the meantime, you'd like to be milked, I daresay. Then I will mash you up a bit of your name, ha!'" Granddad smiles, then frowns. "Never did name her. Do you think Pumpkin might have been a fine name?"

"I think Pumpkin would have been a perfect name!"

"Do you know why I called my home Arrowhead?" Granddad says so loudly I nearly spill my tea. I shake my head.

"As you see, your old granddad was something of a farmer and I plowed a great many fields. Well, can you guess what I found as I planted tomatoes and corn? Arrowheads of course! And I held those relics in my dirt-covered hands and wondered what Mohican man stood on that ground before me, hunting right there. Was my home built atop his?"

Granddad looks at me, his eyes shining. "Would you like to see a real arrowhead, Eleanor?"

"Oh, yes, Granddad. May I?"

Granddad gets up slowly, keeping his woolen shawl around him and moves to his bureau, pulling open a heavy drawer. He peers inside and takes something in his hand.

"Here. Look at this. Feel its weight and imagine the person who chipped it into this shape."

I take the object in my hand. It feels cold and small. It is gray in color and sharp on the edges. To Granddad, it means a lot, so of course it does to me as well.

"You may keep it," he says and kisses my head.

I throw my arms around his middle and hug him tightly.

MOBY-DICK

"Granddad, who is Ishmael?" I ask at the breakfast table. Granddad nearly spills his tea. Grandmamma's eyebrows go up.

"Who is Ishmael?" he repeats my question. "However do you know about Ishmael, child?"

"After our talk I went home to the study where Papa keeps all his books, and there on the shelf was your book, *Moby-Dick*. I pulled it off the shelf. It's heavy, you know."

Granddad laughs. "I know. And...?" he gestures for me to continue.

"Well, I started reading it. That's the first sentence, 'Call me Ishmael.' I wondered who Ishmael was. And I wonder why he likes knocking people's hats off and following funerals." I look quizzically at Granddad.

"Herman, your granddaughter asks a good question. Why *does* he like knocking people's hats off?" My grandmother winks at me, and smiles at Granddad teasingly. Aunt Bessie laughs. He looks flustered. Then he looks deeply into his bowl of oatmeal and stirs it slowly.

I ask again. "Is his *name* Ishmael? He says to *call* him that, but is it his name?"

Granddad scratches his head and then smiles mischievously. "A magician never reveals his secrets."

"But Granddad!"

"It is a question, isn't it?" he says.

"Herman," Grandmamma repeats, "your granddaughter asks a simple question."

Granddad scratches his head and thinks. Everyone is looking at him.

"Why does he like knocking people's hats

off, you ask? Have you never wanted to knock somebody's hat off?"

I haven't and tell him so. "Do you? Do *you* want to knock people's hats off?" I ask him. Sometimes he confuses me.

"On occasion, I admit, I do." Granddad stirs his oats with vigor. "Bessie, bring your old father some more tea." Granddad is getting a bit red under his collar.

Aunt Bessie gets up creakily and kisses Granddad on the top of his head.

"You are a curious girl. So, I will tell you a story of how that big book came to be, if you like. Yes? Good. But first, finish your plate or

Jack Smoke will come down the chimney and take what you leave!"

I quickly finish my porridge.

"You know my birthday is very near..."

"Yes, I know and I have a gift for you," I say, and pat the old man's hand.

"That's wonderful. Well, it was a very special August day, not exactly on my birthday, but close enough, and what I got that year was a very special gift indeed."

"What kind of gift? Did you get a pen? A horse? I wonder if you will like my gift to you."

"No, neither, and I am sure I will love your gift. But on that day, what I got was a friend."

"A friend for a gift? Was he wrapped in paper?" Granddad laughs at my silliness.

"He was not, but he and I had to wrap ourselves up when the rains came tumbling out of the sky, with thunder and lightning to boot!

"A few days after my 31st birthday, as way of celebration, some friends invited me to hike up to the top of Monument Mountain in Great Barrington. I loved to hike and on that hot summer day in August I was still a young man and ready to climb a mountain I had never climbed before. I had heard tales of this mountain, made famous by William Cullen Bryant's poem about the legend of the Indian maiden who had thrown herself off the top in despair, brokenhearted over her love for a cousin." Granddad knows I am a romantic, like him and looks at me, his bushy eyebrows reaching up to his forehead.

"Oh, Granddad! Did she really jump?" I could listen to my grandfather tell stories all day. I imagine what a great writer he must be with all his stories.

"That is a question for historians. Or poets. But I loved hearing these tales and I was intrigued by the thought of a picnic on the mountaintop with other writers. Maybe I would meet her ghost! Actually, I sorely needed a break from my writing."

"What were you working on then?"

"Why, the fat one we have been discussing, about that white whale. I had been at my uncle's house writing that adventure and I needed some fresh air and exercise. My old friend, Oliver Wendell Holmes met us at the base of the mountain and introduced me to the man who would become my best friend, Mr. Nathanial Hawthorne."

"I know who he is!"

"Of course you do, like any literate person should! And I knew his work as well. I was very excited to meet such an excellent writer. And almost better, he knew my books."

"Did he know the one about the whale?"

"No, that was a work in progress, but he knew my *Typee* and he told me he thought it a marvelous tale."

"That is great praise from such an author!"

Granddad looks at me strangely. "What is your age, child?"

"Granddad, I am nine, you know that. We just celebrated my birthday."

"Ah, all this talk of birthdays, I should remember. And you have read my friend, Hawthorne?"

"Mama let me read *A Wonder–Book for Girls & Boys* and then *Tanglewood Tales for Girls & Boys*. I should wish my name were Periwinkle!

I wanted that for myself and for Frances to be called Primrose but Mama refused." Granddad is looking at me comically.

"Well, as the rains came down and the lighting struck, Mr. Hawthorne and I took refuge under the cover of some cave-like rocks, and there, discussed a great many things, my latest work among them. The story I was writing was yet another adventure tale, but I longed to write something else, something more...more epic. He encouraged me, and we had many literary discussions long after this picnic. Sometimes Mr. Hawthorne stopped by Arrowhead and he and I would sit up in the rafters of my barn and smoke cigars and talk and talk."

"Grandmamma let you smoke cigars?"

"Of course she did not." Granddad looks at Grandmamma with a funny little glance.

She smiles. "Of course I did not. I would have none of that pesky cigar smoke in my house. I sent him and Nathaniel to the barn. Like little boys, I dare say."

"Yes, even like Malcolm and Stanwix," Granddad says.

"My uncles? The ones I never knew?"

"The very same." Everyone seems sad then. I know those boys died a long time ago. I think my mother and father would be sad if I died before they did. But Granddad brightens quickly again. "And so I threw out the tale I was working on and re-worked it to what you began in your father's study. *Moby-Dick*. I dedicated the book to him."

"You did? Was he happy? I would be happy if you dedicated a book to me," I say. "But why did you say that no one else wanted to read it? It's so big and interesting and you are such a great writer."

"How do you know that I am a great writer?" my grandfather asks.

"I just do."

Grandmamma Lizzie frowns and says, "Eleanor, that's en...", but then a thought enters my head.

"Granddad," I ask, "Why did you never write a book for your children?"

Granddad frowns so hard his beard seems to get shorter.

"Yes, Papa, why never a book for me and Fanny?" Aunt Bessie winks at me as she asks the question. Granddad is silent for a long time, then he clears his throat like he's about to recite a poem.

"I wrote you little notes, letters, I even illustrated them. Do you remember?"

"Yes, Papa, I still have one from you."

"Oh, Aunt Bessie, will you get it? May I read it?" I want to see what Granddad wrote to her.

"Oh dear, it's up on the third floor and I'm feeling a bit achy today. Would you run and get it?"

"Yes!"

Aunt Bessie tells me where it is and I bound upstairs to get the letter. When I come down, everyone is looking at me.

"You read it aloud, Eleanor, dear," Aunt Bessie says.

I clear my throat like Granddad. "*To Elizabeth Melville, 2 September 1860, Pacific Ocean. My Dear Bessie: I thought I would send you a letter, that you could read yourself — at*

69

least a part of it. But here and there I propose to write in the usual manner, as I find the printing style comes rather awkwardly in a rolling ship. Mama will read these parts to you."

"Which I did," my grandmother interrupts.

I continue. "'We have seen a good many sea-
birds. Many have followed the ship day after day.
I used to feed them with crumbs. But now it has
got to be warm weather, the birds have left us.
They were about as big as chickens – they were all
over speckled – they would sometimes, during a
calm, keep behind the ship, fluttering about in the
water, with a mighty cackling, and whenever anything was thrown overboard they would hurry to
get it. But they would never light on the ship – they
kept all the time flying or else resting themselves by
floating on the water like ducks in a pond. These
birds have no home, unless it is some wild rocks
in the middle of the ocean. They never see any
orchards, and have a taste of the apples & cher-
ries, like your gay little friend in Pittsfield, Robin
Red Breast, Esq.

~I could tell you a good many more things
about the sea, but I must defer the rest till I get
home.

I hope you are a good little girl; and give Mama
no trouble. Do you help Mama keep house? That
little bag you made for me, I use it very often, and
think of you every time.

I suppose you have had a good many walks on the hill, and picked the strawberries.

I hope you take good care of little FANNY and that when you go up the hill, you go this way: that is to say, hand in hand.

By-by

Papa.'

And there's a little drawing you made, Granddad! It's so tiny and darling!"

"I would say that's as good as any book I could have written for my children. Don't you agree?"

I do not, but I just smile and nod my head. Aunt Bessie winks at me, and so does Grandmamma Lizzie. Granddad looks very satisfied.

A Swan Boat Ride
in Central Park

I have been trying to read *Moby-Dick* at home in New Jersey, and it is quite difficult, like Mama said. But at least she lets me try. My father even says I can circle the words I don't understand, but there are too many. It is on my bedside table and makes me feel close to Granddad when I am away from him. But good news, we are leaving New Jersey early this morning for New York and Granddad has promised to take us to the big park in the city. Central Park. So of course, today is my favorite day! Granddad is taking us to ride the Swan Boat.

Mama packs us each a little overnight bag, which makes me heart swell. Going to Granddad's is absolutely my favorite place to go! I am a tiny bit angry that Frances is coming along, but she would be very sad to stay home without her big sister.

The train ride is not even an hour and we walk briskly to 26th Street. Granddad meets us at the door, his cane in his hand. He kisses my mother and pulls Frances and me into a tight hug.

He tells me this is a belated birthday gift, since my birthday is in February and a swan boat ride then would be impossible. It would be ice. Granddad gave me a book for my real birthday. I love it and have looked at the pictures over and over! It is *Landseer's Dogs and Their Stories*. He knows how I love animals, but best of all, he knows how I love the Swan Boat. Granddad was on many boats in his lifetime. I'm sure this is nothing compared to those times, but he's old now and cannot do too many exciting things anymore.

I wish Frances could stay with Grandmamma Lizzie, but she is to come along too, which makes me a little mad and disappointed. She is so young and when she is there, Granddad must pay attention to her and cannot give all his attention to me, and since this is my birthday gift, I would like for my sister to stay behind. Is that ungenerous? That is what Mama says.

The line for the Swan Boat is long today. I wish I could take off my bonnet, it makes me hot, but Mama would be angry if I did. Frances is pulling on hers. She must be hot too. The sun is strong today and I wish I could jump in the lake and cool off.

There is a man with a funny round hat selling peanuts and a boy throwing bits of bread in the lake. Real ducks are fighting for the crumbs.

AROUND THE LAKE 5 CENTS, the sign says and Granddad pulls out a little beaded coin purse and hands it to me. "Pull out a nickel, if you please," he says. I find a nickel at the bottom of the purse and hand it to Granddad. He pays a very bored looking man and we climb aboard.

The front part of the boat is covered with a canopy, and it is nice and shady there with room for many people, but the Swan boat is attached behind it and only has room for two. Or three, since Frances is so small. Even

though we will be hotter here with no cover, Granddad knows I want to sit right in the Swan. It's my birthday gift.

He sits between Frances and me, wrapping us up in his arms. It feels nice to sit here as the boat goes 'round the small lake.

"Granddad, what was it like being on a big boat?"

Granddad laughs and squeezes me more tightly. "Nothing like this, I can say that!"

"Did you get seasick?"

"Well, on my first trip, I must admit I did! But once I got my sea legs I never again had to give up my meals to the sea. And sometimes the storms were enough to make you dizzy, but your granddad has a stomach of iron. The waves were so high and so rough, the wind so boisterous, that some of my shipmates could barely set foot on deck, but not your old granddad."

"Weren't you scared?" I know I would have been, but I will not think of that and would never tell Granddad. He thinks I am a brave girl, and so I must be.

"Scared? Oh, there were times I thought, 'this is my last day on earth. I will be swimming with the whales,' but here I am still." He squeezes my shoulder.

"I'm glad you are, but Granddad, did you ever see a whale?"

"Many and many. And participated in killing them too, I'm sorry to tell you. They are the grandest creatures ever to swim the seas. In fact, they are indeed the grandest creatures on earth."

"I know whales are big. I heard the story of Jonah, from the Bible."

"I'm sure you did." Granddad will not read the Bible anymore, but he must know that story.

"Can you catch one with a fishing pole?" my silly sister asks.

Granddad laughs heartily. "I should say not. They are bigger than any ship I've ever sailed upon and could kill a man with one blow of their tail."

My sister hides her face in Granddad's coat. "That's a big fish, Grandda," my sister says.

"Whales are not fish; did you not learn that in your school?"

"Granddad, Frances is not yet in school. But whales swim and live in the sea!"

"Whales are mammals, like you and me. Warm blooded, and I should know. They have calves like cows do and their calves suckle the same way. And they're smart. Some smarter than a man." Granddad looks at me as if daring me to argue. I do not.

"Where did you sleep?"

"If you can call it that, I slept in a bunk, made of rough wood, like a shelf. A smelly, uncomfortable shelf. But the sea rocked me like a babe in a cradle, the sea, our mother rocking us to sleep. Did you know that when I returned to land, I had terrible trouble getting to sleep in a bed? I slept on the floor! Getting my land legs back was always a challenge."

"Can girls go to sea, Granddad?"

"I never heard of one, certainly not New Jersey girls. But the Marquesan girls all knew how to paddle a canoe. Yes, they did." He

looks pensive again, as if remembering something he would rather forget.

"Where is Mar...mark...?"

"The Marquesas? They are far away in the South Pacific, where the waters are bluer than any sky you could wish to see, and the sand is soft and warm beneath your toes."

"You went without your shoes?"

"Of course I did. The natives practically went without clothing." He laughs.

I am afraid to ask, but I do. "Did you as well?"

"Me? Unclad? No, dear Eleanor, but I did swim with only my breeches."

"Is it hot there, Granddad?"

"Hot and loud with birdsong and insect song and singing and chanting and laughter..." His voice trails off and he looks up at the sun. His old face is crisscrossed with wrinkles, but his blue eyes are sparkling. He closes them and I think he must be remembering something. I want to ask him what, but he looks so pleasant, that I just rest my head against his arm. Maybe here is where his secret lies. I wish I could peek inside his thoughts and find it.

Granddad opens his eyes again and waves his arm about like a conductor. "But here we are. Just look at this park, Eleanor and Frances, with its greenery and this little lake. It is a little piece of paradise here in this metropolis. Just look there," he points. "Do you see the jay? Look at that bright blue wing. And the crow there, see how his wings shimmer in the sun. It's good here."

Is Granddad convincing himself?

"Do you miss those places Granddad?"

"Miss them! No indeed! Had I stayed, I would have been a marked man, and I mean that in the most literal sense of the word. They would have marked me in ink. Tattoos, I mean. The Marquesans are marked, some of them from head to toe, face and all. Mind you, they are some of the best artists I have ever seen."

"Girls too?"

"Girls, boys, women and men. It is tradition, and one that we shall never adopt in this world, but there, it is the most important thing a person can do."

"My sister has a tattoo, don't you Frances?"

"Look Grandda!" she says, showing her tattooed finger.

Just last year, Granddad told Frances a story about the cannibals he met in the Pacific. He had pulled up his sleeve and showed her his tattoo, "made by the very cannibals." I was not there to see it, but I believe he had cunningly drawn it right before my sister arrived. She told me it was a star and can you imagine what she did when she got home? She punctured her finger with a needle and put ink into the wound! Now she has a tattoo! And Mama calls me reckless and headstrong!

Granddad laughs deeply and shakes his head. "Your mother will never forgive me for that. You shall be the only girl in New York with such an emblem! Keep it hidden child, or you will never get a husband."

And with that, he takes Frances upon his lap. I snuggle closer to Granddad, wishing Frances were not here. I should be on his lap. It's my birthday after all.

GRANDDAD HERMAN
AND THE SEA

Granddad must have enjoyed my questions because he is telling me more about his time at sea. I am thrilled and breathless as he describes it.

"Eleanor, come and sit with me and watch the tall ships. Just look at those sails!" Pointing with his cane, he says, "And see the little boats sailing hither and thither." Granddad is funny sometimes.

We sit on a bench at the South Street Seaport, his favorite place in New York, and watch the tall ships sail in and out of the harbor. Granddad always breathes deeply when we come here. It smells like fish and salt. He likes the smell better than I do, but I breathe with him. Once I breathed so fast and deeply, I felt dizzy. The sails are white and made of canvas. They sound very loud as they move in the wind.

"Why did you go to sea, Granddad?"

"My father intrigued me with his tales of the sea. On winter evenings, by the well-remembered sea-coal fires in old Greenwich Street, he used to tell my brother and me tales of the monstrous waves at sea, mountain-high, and of the masts bending like twigs."

"And you liked that? That would have frightened me tremendously."

Granddad only laughs.

"And was your father, my great-grandfather, telling the truth?"

"That and more. Waves as tall as mountains, yes, whales bigger than your imagination, sharks circling our ships, ready to taste anyone unlucky enough to lose his

footing. Oh, yes, my father may have been many things, but when it came to the sea, he was honest as the salt itself."

Granddad looks distant as if searching for a memory. I can almost see the wild waves reflected in his dark eyes.

"I remember it like yesterday, that sea voyage. The wind was bracing as I set foot on the deck. The air smelled sharply of salt, penetrating my nostrils and clearing my head of any thoughts of school or family or disgrace. I took in the scene about me. Rough gray water, the land disappearing, the sky large and seemingly endless. Waves sloshed over the side of the ship, soaking my boots. I felt the cold wet seep through the hard leather, into my socks, chilling my feet."

"I would not like water getting in my boots!" I think that sounds dreadful and very uncomfortable.

"Nor did I. The January day was frigid but I knew that the days would grow warmer as we headed south. But this would be my life for months. Wet, salty, sticky and cold."

"Didn't you mind?"

"Mind? It was often very uncomfortable, but I loved being at sea. I loved the smell of the salt air, the bracing wind. I was twenty-one, young and strong. I had been a cabin boy on the merchant ship St. Lawrence and had crossed the Atlantic, so I knew about the cold but knew nothing about whaling, and as I may have said..."

"You loved adventure!"

"I gather I might have said such before," Granddad laughs deep from his belly.

"I'll tell you a story, if you don't think it will bore you, dear Eleanor."

"Of course it won't bore me, Granddad."

"As I said, when I was a young man, only twenty-one, I signed on to a whaling ship, *The Acushnet* from Fairhaven, Massachusetts. The seas were rough and wild, like my father had told me. And once or twice, I feared for our lives, but Captain Pease was an able sailor, and though he was irascible, he kept us from harm. Mostly though, I drank in the sea air, like a tonic.

"*The Acushnet* was a strong vessel, a whaler. Working on a merchant ship was nothing compared with being crew on a whaler, but I was ready to be on the waves again."

"My friend Toby Green was there with me, so I had a companion to talk to on those lonely days when all you see is gray. We were looking for whales and found many too, I can tell you. But I won't go into those details, you might be disturbed."

I nod my head, but don't speak. Granddad continues.

"There were nights wild with weather, storms at sea and days so calm and windless you could see your own reflection in the liquid silver."

"Did you dive in?"

"Indeed I did! We all did on those hot windless days. The doldrums. Had to watch for sharks, but it was glorious, though we always wanted wind. We had to wait until the wind picked up to move on and sometimes it took days. Put the captain in a terrible temper.

"I had no idea what lay ahead. Chasing whales in the middle of the ocean was a treacherous business at best. One had to be strong of body and of wit to endure the grueling hours of waiting and watching, and then killing the giant beasts. Many a man had been killed or maimed in this pursuit. Does that shock you, my dear?"

"A little. But Granddad, why did you kill whales? Did you not feel pity for them?"

"I did indeed. It was not glamorous and it was cruel, I admit. We killed them for their oil. It was a very profitable business.

"I had read books about whales. I knew they were large mammals, the largest on the planet and that they would bring in oil and money and best of all, adventure."

"I know you love adventure so much, but I feel sad for the whales."

Granddad pats me on the head, but says nothing.

"Tell me more, Granddad."

He smiles at me and nods.

"I had heard so many tales of the sea, most especially that of the whaling ship *Essex*, which sank in 1820 when I was only a year old. The story of the great Sperm whale that sunk that ship stayed with me. I needed to see for myself, firsthand, what a whaling ship was about. I wanted adventure, and I was sure to find it on board this ship.

"Captain Pease was an ornery character, rough and surly, like a character in a Gothic horror. I did not like the man from the start for when he was in a bad temper, everyone on board felt it. I hoped I could stand being in such close quarters, but I tried, as we all did to keep out of the captain's way. Even that was hard."

"Why was that hard? On a big ship?"

"The ship is not so big as to hide from that man. For one thing, you could smell him from anywhere on deck, above or below. He reeked constantly of sickeningly sweet lotions. That combined with salt and sweat was unbearable." Granddad makes a funny face and holds his nose closed. "I grew tired of hearing the other sailors complaining about the captain. And we all tried to avoid him, ducking beneath the yardarm, the far end of the ship or scurrying below deck. And he would yell!"

"What would he yell?"

Granddad puts on a gruff voice, "'Where are you sailors? Do you hear me! Stand ho! Come on deck!' he would bellow. Unnerved me, I can tell you." I love when he puts on voices.

"When did you see whales, Granddad?"

"As the days went by and the waters became warmer, we began to spot the great beasts. 'WHALE HO!' the sailors called.

"I could see their smooth dark bodies skimming the surface of the water. One breached." Granddad stops and looks at me. "Do you know what that means?"

I shake my head.

"Oh, Eleanor, it's a sight! The leviathan comes up out of the water in a great show of acrobatics, some nearly all the way out of the water, then turns and slaps down as it dives below. It is a most incredible sight."

"Weren't you frightened the whale should splash your boat and knock you overboard?"

"How did you guess? We all gasped as we watched the colossal creature rise up, then smack down hard as he dove back down creating tidal waves. But mostly I thought about what would come next. Killing the magnificent beasts for oil. I felt sick, but knew I had no choice. The captain was crazy for oil, and this was, after all, a whaling ship."

I squeeze my eyes shut. I cannot bear to think of the poor whales. Granddad pats my head again.

"I thought of the great whale from *the Essex*. I knew the whales would fight for their lives and I hoped everyone on board would be safe. Wouldn't you know it, after months out on sea, deep in the Pacific, the *Acushnet* met another whaling ship. On that ship, I encountered a teenage boy, William Henry Chase. I recognized the name. Chase's father, Owen Chase had been aboard the *Essex* and had survived to tell the tale! Owen Chase had written a small book telling the story and William gave his only copy to me. I read it, fascinated by the gruesome tale."

"Is that what your whale book is about? I haven't gotten very far."

Granddad laughs. "Not exactly, child." Granddad pauses for just a moment, then continues, "After more than a year, Toby and I grew tired of Captain Pease's temper, and we decided to jump ship in the South Pacific."

"Granddad! You jumped overboard?"

"No, I say that figuratively. We found ourselves in Nukahiva, on an island in the Marquesas. Oh, the Marquesas! What strange visions of outlandish things did the name spirit up in me! Cannibal banquets, cocoa-nut, coral reefs, tattooed chiefs – and bamboo temples; sunny valleys planted with breadfruit, tree-carved canoes dancing on the flashing blue waters!"

I can hardly believe this from the old man.

"Granddad, and was it like your imaginings?"

"Even more so. As we approached I saw the green land, with its rocky headlands and lush waterfalls and I knew then, I needed to get away from Captain Pease and the whole grueling voyage, cannibals or no.

"As the *Acushnet* neared the land, we heard strange outcries, and there from the shore came a flotilla of native canoes. They made one devil of a sound! Such grunts and shouts! One of my shipmates stood by me and pointed, 'There, matey, there's the Typee. Oh, the bloody cannibals, what a meal they'd make of us if we were

to take it into our heads to land!'

"Little did he know I was about to make my escape. Toby longed to get off the boat too, and so we later stuffed as much hardtack as we could carry and slipped away and traversed through the jungle and climbed mountains that were actually volcanoes. Are you shocked?"

I am breathless as he weaves this tale. I know he loves adventure, but I did not know my grandfather was such an adventurer as this.

"A little."

Granddad laughs deeply. "Shall I continue?"

"Oh, yes! Please."

"We tried to stay clear of the native people, but I hurt my leg and became very sick. We walked for many days until I couldn't walk with my pain, fever and chills. 'Toby,' I had groaned to my friend. 'I can't move another foot. My head feels like the pounding of the waves and I'm about as hot as the equatorial sun.' Toby had put his hand on my brow and pulled back, it was so hot. I was raging with fever."

"Oh! Granddad!"

"Yes, I had a fever that might have taken my life had it not been for…"

"Toby? He saved you, didn't he?"

Granddad looks stern. "Toby? Why, no. He abandoned me. No, it was the Typee who saved me."

"The cannibals you were afraid of?"

"The very ones."

"Did they try to eat you?!"

"They saved my life and took me in. Fed me cocoa-nuts and breadfruit."

"But why did Toby abandon you? I never would have." I am angry with Toby Greene.

"Toby promised to get help. Now, now, don't be angry with him," Granddad chuckles, seeing my balled-up fists and red face. "He really tried. 'I will get help! You are sick, friend, very sick!' I could have told you that, I had said. Then I told him to go and fetch me some water. And that was the last I saw of my friend, until many years later."

"Did he say sorry when you met him again? I hope he did."

"Yes, he did, and he actually was sorry. He wanted to return to me, but he had been shanghaied onto an Australian whaler."

"What is shanghaied?"

"That means he was forced aboard. You see, he could not return, Instead, I was left to the care of the Typee, who never had any intention of eating me; instead, they wanted to induct me into their society. I might have married one of the beautiful Marquesan girls...don't whisper a word to your grand-mother. Fayaway would have had me." He looks pensive again.

"Was she pretty, Granddad?"

"She was pretty indeed. Beautiful, in fact. Long hair as black as the deepest sea, eyes as dark. She spoke her language as if it were a song. And strong! She helped to carry me when I was ill, and I am a big fellow."

"Did you want to marry her?"

"Marry her? That would have been out of the question. No, dear child, I was such a young man, and so inexperienced in the ways of love and marriage, but I loved her in my way. And she loved me. And that is that. As I requested, do not mention a word to your grandmother. Understand?"

"I can keep a secret, Granddad, really I can." Granddad nods. He knows I am to be trusted.

Was this the secret? Of course, I will keep it. I think it's dreadfully romantic and would never tell my grandmother. Not even my sister or my mother. Is he still pining for her? That makes me feel a little sad for Grandmamma, but also makes me curious about Granddad as a young man. I imagine him as a handsome sailor in love with a dark-haired mermaid.

"After a while, I became well and strong again and I learned much about the life and traditions of my new friends. The men were hunters and fishermen. They went out on longboats together, rowing in unison, making loud grunting sounds as they rowed. You might have been afraid to hear them. They nearly barked."

"I would not be afraid."

"You are a brave girl. The girls of the islands were also brave and strong. They climbed trees and collected cocoa-nuts and tropical fruits. They cleaned and cooked the fish over open fires. Delicious! They swam in the sea. They splashed and laughed and played, even the adults. I enjoyed them and their company. They prayed over the fire and over the rocks and over the sea. Their religion became mine. The religion of the natural world."

I know Granddad will not go to church. Mama makes me go. I don't mind, but sometimes I wish I could stay with Granddad on a Sunday morning.

"After four months, the Marquesans decided that I should be part of the tribe and set to adopt me. Which meant to mark me."

"*Tattoo* you?"

"That was the intention. And so, in the middle of a bright tropical afternoon, I left."

"Did they look for you?"

"I would imagine. They wanted me to be a son or brother, and had it not been for the markings, I might have stayed a while longer. It was a beautiful place, free from the confines of the city, from religion, from conservative views of life. It was open and free, so unlike the society I had grown up in. Never a stuffy moment; no parlors with tea and tedious conversation. But I go on! Dear Eleanor, you must think your old granddad mad."

I think my granddad to be the very best person I know. And I tell him so.

"I found another whaler, the *Julia* out of Australia. That was an adventure all its own. The crew, and me now an unwitting member, staged a mutiny and your granddad wound up in jail in Tahiti for three months! Calabooza Beretanee. English jail. Captain Bob was our lackadaisical jailer, and the guards were always asleep, so one day I simply walked out and hopped on another boat, which took me to Hawaii."

I am breathless from my grandfather's adventures and a little envious.

"Do you not like land, Granddad? I thought you loved the mountains." Sometimes Granddad perplexes me.

"I do love the mountains. I love nature in general, but a young man must experience all sorts of terrains and different horizons. The mountains would be there when I returned and so they were."

"What about a young woman? Might she not want to experience new places too?"

Granddad looks at me with a puzzled expression. I think I might like to see new places, not always New Jersey and New York.

"Finally I had had enough of the sea faring life but I had to get home somehow. I joined the U.S. Navy and boarded the frigate ship the *United States*. It was there that I began telling my stories to any who would listen. I wove a fine tale, I must say, and the sailors never tired of my stories. Of course, there was not much else to do on such a long voyage, and by the time I arrived home some three years later in 1844, I was so well-versed in story telling that I so entertained my family with my tales that they encouraged me to write them down."

"And you did!"

"I did indeed. Typee and Omoo were my first novels and they were very successful, I must admit."

"May I read them?"

"Oh, I think your mother will forbid that until you are a grown woman."

"But why, Granddad?"

"Too many scantily clad natives. Fayaway. Too much adventure for a proper New Jersey girl. But here, don't look so, you can read

them in my study while I doze. I'll not tell if you don't." He winks at me.

I smile again and Granddad pats my head.

"And then you met your wife, my grandmother?"

"Yes, about that time. I had gone to Boston to visit my father's old friend, Lemuel Shaw, Chief Justice of the Massachusetts Supreme Court, your great-grandfather. Well, he had a lovely daughter, Elizabeth…"

"Grandmamma Lizzie?"

"That's the one. She loved hearing my tales of sea voyages and cannibals. We fell in love and married three years later, soon after my novel Typee had been published."

Granddad stands up quickly as if he just remembered something he forgot. He pulls his blue coat about him and his hat down on his head. "Let's get home, the wind is blowing up a gale."

The tall sails are bucking back and forth in the wind, the boats rocking. I hear granddad say something as we get up from the bench, it's almost a whisper, but I am sure he says, "And I have work to do."

I wonder what work he has to do. He doesn't work anymore. Does this work have something to do with his secret? I am desperate to know.

SHHH, GRANDDAD IS WRITING

I cannot sleep, all this talk of whales and tattoos. The room is very dark and my sister is snoring. I want to talk to Granddad, so I sneak out of bed, put on my slippers and my robe and quietly leave our little room. There is soft light from Aunt Bessie's room next door and I wonder what she is doing in there, so late at night.

I have no candle, so I feel my way down toward Granddad's study, where I hope he is still awake. I see light coming from under the doorway and I open it, ever so quietly. I see Granddad, but his back is to me. I am very quiet and I am about to speak, but Granddad is talking aloud, his quill pen scribbling away. There is no one else in the room, so I imagine he is talking to himself. I have never heard him do this before.

"*Don't know where you were born?—Who was your father?*" Granddad speaks, then scribbles with his quill. He continues.

"*God knows, Sir.*" And he writes this too, I am guessing.

He continues writing as he speaks the next, "*Do you know anything about your beginning?*"

"*No, Sir. But I have heard that I was found in a pretty silk lined basket hanging one morning from the knocker of a good man's door in Bristol.*" More scribbling.

"*Found say you? Well,*" *throwing back his head and looking up and down the new recruit;* "*Well, it turns out to have been a pretty good find. Hope they'll find some more like you, my man; the fleet sadly needs them.*"

Yes, Billy Budd was a foundling, a presumable by-blow, and, evidently, no ignoble one.

Noble descent was as evident in him as in a blood horse.'"

Granddad writes some more then puts down his quill and pulls his fingers through his thick hair. He leans back in his chair. I have been so quiet that he still does not know I am here. I am not sure if I should make myself known, but then Granddad seems to hear my thoughts and spins around.

"Eleanor, it is late! Why are you awake, child? Come here." He pats his knee for me to sit upon. I do. I lean back on him and breathe in his scent. It is a familiar and pleasant smell, like peppermint and wood smoke.

He strokes my head.

"Could not sleep?"

I yawn and nod.

"Me neither."

"Granddad, I heard you talking. Who were you talking to? Who is Billy Budd?"

"To myself, dear child. I often speak aloud when I am writing. Helps the words come." He pauses. "Who is Billy Budd, you ask? You do pay attention. Hmmn? He is a sailor; a young and handsome sailor."

"Like you once were?"

"Once upon a time."

"Are you writing a new story, Granddad?"

"I am, and I'm nearly done, but you mustn't tell, especially your grandmother."

Suddenly my mind makes a little jump. This is Granddad's secret! My heart feels about to burst. It is beating as if I have been running fast. I will never tell.

"I promise I won't tell, Granddad. I will keep your secret."

"Good girl. You keep Billy Budd's name to yourself and I will be proud of you. No one needs know. It will be our secret."

"Oh Granddad, you can trust me. I won't tell Mama or Frances and especially Grandmamma Lizzie."

"Is this too much of a burden for you, dear Tittery-Eye? Do I ask too much?"

I shake my head, happy to be called Granddad's pet name for me and snuggle close to my favorite person. I must have fallen asleep there in Granddad's arms, for the next thing I know my grandfather is tucking me into my bed.

KEEP TRUE TO THE
DREAMS OF THY YOUTH

My cousin Agnes is here visiting! She is a bit older than I am and our favorite thing to do when she comes for a visit is to jump on Grandmamma's bed!

"Let's jump on Aunt Lizzie's bed!" she says as soon as she puts down her suitcase. For some reason, I don't understand, Grandmamma allows this, but only when Agnes is here.

Today, Grandmamma is sitting in her chair watching us jump up and down on her white bed. It squeaks and creaks. I wonder if she wishes to hop on with us. That's what Granddad once told me. He thought his own mother wanted to climb trees. But my grandmother is too old to jump on the bed. Frances climbs on and I try to shoo her off. She begins to cry, so I let her. Little sisters are very vexatious.

"What's all this? Jumping on the bed like monkeys?" Granddad pretends to be angry with us when he comes into the room.

"It's fun, Grandda!" yells Frances.

"Fun."

"What's that in your hand?" I ask him. I see he is holding a little rose-bud china pitcher.

"Nothing for you, child. This is for your grandmother."

I hop down off the bed and run over to him.

"May I see it? It's pretty. I will give it to her," I say and reach for the gift.

"You will not. I will give it to my wife, thank you." And he stands before my grandmother and gives her the little trinket.

We all watch him, wondering why he wants to give her this gift. Is it their anniversary? But no, it is not. And I feel a little sorry for myself that Granddad has admonished me.

But then I remember; he is a romantic, like me.

"Let's leave the lovebirds alone," my cousin giggles.

We go into our room and jump on Frances' bed.

Later, after Agnes has gone back to her home, I find Granddad in his study.

"I'm sorry Granddad for trying to take away your pleasure. I like to give gifts too."

"I forgive you, Tittery-Eye. Sometimes a husband has to give a gift to his wife. One day you will understand that."

I'm not sure I will, but I agree.

"Remember, dear Eleanor, I am old, but haven't forgotten what I once was. Here, look at this." Granddad takes a small piece of paper from his writing desk and hands it to me. It reads, *Keep True to the Dreams of Thy Youth.* The paper is old and worn and seems to live there inside his traveling desk.

"Never forget this time, when you are young and your dreams are fresh and new. If you can keep these words in your heart, you will always be young here." He pats his own heart. "You might even want to still jump on your bed when you are an old woman!"

"Do *you* ever want to jump on the bed?"

"The idea has crossed my mind once or twice."

The image of Granddad jumping on his big black bed makes me giggle! Granddad holds up the note, showing me.

"I won't forget Granddad. If you can remember your life, from the time you were a little boy, even younger than I am now, I will press all my memories into my heart and keep them there for later. For forever."

"Yes, dear Eleanor, you do that. Then you will be able to tell your children and your grandchildren, who will then be my great-great-great grandchildren, about your life. That's a funny thought. And they will tell theirs and we will always stay alive in hearts and minds. And those dreams that we dream in our youth will also stay alive."

"I love you, Granddad."

"And I you, Tittery-Eye."

HERMAN MELVILLE DIES

It is raining in my heart today because Granddad has died. Just seven months and four days after my ninth birthday, this quite special grandfather has died. Mama told me when I came downstairs for breakfast. I could see she had been crying. Her eyes were red rimmed and very shimmery. One tear slipped down her face when she told me.

She sniffled and said, "Eleanor, your granddad has left us."

I wanted to say, left us for where!? For Arrowhead? For that is what I wished. But

I knew what she meant. I did not want it to be true.

"You don't have to attend school today, my dear. We will go to the city and comfort Grandmamma Lizzie."

But I need comfort. I need my granddad to comfort me. To pull me close so I can snuggle up to him, smelling the woodsmoky scent of him. I think my tears started to flow when I thought about that.

The ride to the city is not at all as the other rides have been. This ride holds not a bit of excitement. Everything looks dull from my window seat. Drab and gray. I don't want to think about my grandfather never again telling me stories, never kissing me on the top of my head, or putting me on his lap so I can pull on his beard.

I love Grandmamma, but never so much as Granddad. Frances and Grandmamma Lizzie are better suited. Frances likes it better in Grandmamma's bright and cheery room, but I prefer to be with my granddad, no matter what room. Granddad is mine. Was mine. My heart might just crack in half, so heavy it is today.

Frances is quiet and Mama is weeping softly. My father, who never likes to come to New York is patting her hand and whispering to her.

The house is dark when we arrive. Cloths cover all the mirrors. I want to ask why, but I do not. The Grandfather clock tells the wrong time and is not ticking.

Everyone is somber. Grandmamma Lizzie hugs my mother tightly and then puts her arms around Frances and me. She squeezes us harder than she ever has before. She lets go, and then backs up to look closely at us, as if she has never really looked at us before. Her face is red and swollen; her eyes watery like my mother's.

Aunt Bessie comes down the stairs slowly. I run to her and she puts her arms around me. I am sure her poor hands are hurting, but she hugs me tightly all the same.

"Oh, Aunt Bessie!"

"I know my darling. I know. I feel the same as you. He loved you well, you must not ever forget that."

"I never will!" I promise Aunt Bessie and myself. And Granddad.

Somewhere in the house is my grandfather. He will be like one of the statues that Frances is so afraid of. Lifeless. All his luster gone away. I think I do not want to see him, but I also want to. I want to say goodbye.

Everyone is somber. We go into the dining

room and have something to eat, but nothing tastes good. Just bland and tasteless.

"Mother, what was he working on? Do you know?" my mother asks her mother.

"Something I was not privy to, and I will not allow another critic to get his hands on it."

I gasp. I want to tell them that I know what Granddad was working on! That he discussed it with me! *Billy Budd*, I want to yell, but I say nothing. I will keep my word to my grandfather. I recall our conversation,

"Are you writing a new book, Granddad?"

"I am, I'm nearly done, but you mustn't tell, especially your grandmother. She wants me to stop this silly habit of mine and stick to poetry that no one understands.

"Is this too much of a burden for you, dear Tittery-Eye? Do I ask too much?"

No, Granddad, not too much. Never too much for you.

Now I am crying hard as I remember his silly name for me. Tittery-Eye. Everyone is looking at me. I pull my napkin off my lap and to my face and hide from them.

My grandmother gets up quite quickly and goes into kitchen. When she comes back she is holding a tin breadbox. Her face is set. The faces of Mama, Papa and Aunt Bessie look like questions. Grandmamma stands at her place at the table, but says nothing and we are all looking at her, wondering why she is standing here holding a breadbox. There is already bread on the table. But she does not put it down, instead she marches out of the room. What is she up to?

Everyone stays in the dining room, but I follow her. She goes into Granddad's study. Why is she bringing that breadbox in there? I hear Grandmamma talking to herself. It makes me feel a little odd. I tiptoe quietly through the door after her. The office is dark and feels so empty. Granddad's big chair looks lost without its occupant and I feel the same. Lost.

Grandmamma is looking for something on the desk. She is rustling papers.

"No one will see what Herman was working on. No one." She says to herself, not to me. I'm not even sure she knows I have followed her here.

She pulls open a heavy drawer. "Aha. Here it is. I knew he was working on something. Did you know too, Eleanor?"

The question surprises me. I thought she didn't realize I was there. "No," I say quickly. "No, Grandmamma, I didn't know." I tell a lie and cross my fingers behind my back. I wonder if it is worse telling a lie or telling a secret, but I promised Granddad and I will never break that promise.

Grandmamma gathers up all the papers into a rustling pile and opens the breadbox, placing them gently inside. Then she looks at me with her finger to her lips. Another secret. Another promise. I nod my head.

"Leave me, child. Leave me to sit here in my husband's chair and perhaps feel him one last time." A tear slides down her wrinkly cheek. And another slides down mine.

Goodbye Granddad

We are all dressed in black as we arrive at Woodlawn Cemetery. This is where they will put Granddad. He is in a box, like Billy Budd is now. I hate the thought of Granddad in a box where he can't see the pine trees or smell the sea.

I wonder if he does those things in heaven, where I am sure he must be by now. Does he see me? If he does, he will see me crying. I can't seem to stop, for I cry every time I think of him and I think of him all the time. He would tell me to wipe my tears and smile for him, but I do not want to.

Mama is holding tightly to my hand as they lower the big box that holds Granddad into the ground. Her hand squeezes mine tightly as the minister is saying his words. Papa is holding Frances whose head is on his shoulder. She won't look. Grandmamma Lizzie and Aunt Bessie are holding on to each other.

From the corner of my eye, I see a man with a notepad. He is taking down notes and looking at us. Is he a reporter? I hope he does not speak to Grandmamma. She is grim. If he is a reporter, I hope he will say only nice and good things about Granddad. That he was a great writer.

When I think of that, I think about Billy Budd in his tin box, secreted away. But where is the breadbox? Where has Grandmamma hidden it?

I have looked and looked, but I cannot find it. I want to ask my grandmother, but she looks so dour I dare not.

Aunt Bessie puts a flower onto Granddad's grave. She gives me one to place there too. Goodbye Granddad, I say as I drop the rose onto the dark wooden box. I will never forget you. In my mind, I hear my grandfather's voice. Nor I you, Tittery Eye.

When the dirt goes over the box, my tears fall freely. People put stones over the dirt. Mama does and so do Papa and Grandmamma Lizzie. Frances still won't look.

We all go back to 26th Street and people have brought food. I am not hungry.

I sneak into Granddad's study. It is dark and empty still. I move to the desk and take a seat in Granddad's big chair. I close my eyes and pretend I am sitting on his lap. In my mind, I pull his beard and snuggle in close. I feel a light kiss on the top of my head.

When I open my eyes, I look down at the dark wooden writing desk. There in the corner is a tiny piece of faded paper sticking out from the corner. I pull it out ever so gently. It is the paper Granddad showed me just a few weeks ago. "Keep true to the dreams of thy youth."

"I will, Granddad. I will." And I tuck the paper into the pocket of my pinafore.

Epilogue
Billy Budd in the Breadbox

Dear Reader,

I left you when I was nine and my grandfather had died. My heart stayed broken for a long time. I missed my grandfather. I know we all must die, but I would have liked him to have seen me grow up and to meet his great-grandsons. But, perhaps he watched us all from heaven. Perhaps he is watching still. And I did live my life. I grew up and married, (I know I said I never would and that I would go to sea) but I fell in love and married and had two sons.

As I grew, I read **all** the books Granddad had written. *Moby Dick*, that fat one about the whale, *Mardi*, *Redburn*, *Pierre*, *White Jacket*, even *Typee* and *Omoo*; the adventures with cannibals, and many more. I learned so much about my grandfather from reading all those books. And reading them made me feel close to him.

I tell my boys and I will tell you, if you are lucky enough to have your grandparents, ask them questions. Ask them about their lives. They are a living, breathing history lesson.

When my grandmother died, some fifteen years after Granddad, I was a woman of twenty-four.

Do you remember that tin breadbox? I certainly did. For many years, I wondered where my grandmother had hidden it. I remembered that sad day Grandmamma Lizzie put Granddad's papers into that box. And then like all memories, it faded a bit and resurfaced from time to time. There were a few times I almost asked my grandmother about it, but she was often forgetful near the end of her life, and I had no thought to disturb her.

When she died, the box passed to Aunt Bessie and my mother, and do you know where we found that old thing? In the attic. Yes, my grandmother had hidden the box up in the attic of the old house.

My mother and Aunt Bessie knew that I was the one most interested in Herman Melville, my grandfather, and so gave the tin breadbox to me. I remember my hands shaking as I opened the lid and saw there my beloved grandfather's work. Poems, letters, and there on the pile was his last manuscript, *Billy Budd*. Oh, how my heart leapt. I could almost feel my granddad next to me, whispering, "Read it, my dear Eleanor, you may read it now."

I took it with me, and Reader, I read it and I read it again. It was near to completion and it was wonderful!

At the same time, Mr. Raymond Weaver was writing a biography of my dear grandfather. I was helping him with all that I knew of

Herman Melville. With his help, we edited it to completion.

And then, Reader, we had it published. And do you know what! It was a grand success. People began to remember my grandfather. And they began reading his work, especially, that big one about the whale, *Moby-Dick*.

And now everyone knows the name of Herman Melville, and it is all because of a precious little book that my grandmother hid in a tin breadbox in the attic of the house on 26th Street that once more found the light of day.

The End

Historical Notes and Other Musings by Jana Laiz

Thank you for reading this story. I hope you liked it and learned a few things.

I wrote this little book in Herman Melville's study on Holmes Road in Pittsfield, MA, sitting at his table, looking out his fairy window. You might ask, really? Is that true? How can that be? Well, I am the very first Writer-in-Residence there, which means since Herman left Arrowhead in 1863, no one has written at his table, looking out his fairy window, until I arrived. This is the biggest honor of my life and gives me the unique privilege to sit in the seat of a literary giant. Every time I enter that room I get goose bumps. And I always ask Herman to help me as I write, and I believe he does.

Here are some fun facts about Herman Melville that I may not have included, but in case you ever have a test on Mr. Melville, you might want to have these facts in your pockt.

Herman was born August 1, 1819 in New York City to Allan Melvill (you see there is no silent 'e' at the end of his name) and Maria Gansevoort Melville (you see there is a silent 'e' at the end of her name.)

We think Maria added the 'e' after Allan died, so that the creditors would not associate her with him, but we're not sure. I just think it's a fun fact.

He was the third of eight children. He had three brothers and four sisters. Gansevoort (1815-1846), Helen (1817-1888), Augusta (1821-1876), Allan (1823-1872), Catherine (1825-1905), Frances (1827-1885) and Thomas (1830-1884).

The month of August was a special time for Herman. He was born on August 1st, he married on August 4th and met Nathanial Hawthorne on August 5th.

When Herman moved to Arrowhead in 1850, there was no porch on any side of the house. The warm, sunny south side of the house would have been the most sensible location for a porch, but Herman looked to the north side and saw "Charlemagne" ~

Mount Greylock, the mountain that inspired him. His neighbors thought he was crazy, but he built a porch or a "piazza" as he called it, there on the north side of the house. And many times, while gazing at that mountain, he would spot a shining light and he would think to himself, Fairies there. Herman knew that magic of that mountain.

Herman and Lizzie often visited their dear friend Sarah Morewood who lived at Broadhall, Uncle Thomas' old house, which is across the field from Arrowhead. (It's now the Pittsfield Country Club.) Sarah was a poet and writer. She loved to have parties and Herman and Lizzie loved to attend her costume balls. Herman would often dress as a sea captain, Lizzie as Mount Greylock. Sarah was very dear to both Herman and Lizzie.

There is a little tea set at Arrowhead that Herman bought long ago. It is a tiny set, just big enough for little hands to hold. The story goes that a traveling salesman came to call with his wares. He was selling kitchen things and tea sets. He had a miniature model and he tried to sell Herman the grown-up sized set, but Herman said, no, he wanted *that* one, because he had little girls that were just the right size for such a tea set.

Herman loved and was inspired by many places in the Berkshires. The Melville Trail is a list of places he loved best. Besides Arrowhead, he loved Park Square in Pittsfield, Hancock Shaker Village, Crane Museum of Paper Making, Balance Rock in Lanesborough, the Lenox Court House, Pontoosuc Lake in Pittsfield, Tanglewood/Hawthorne Cottage, October Mountain and, of course, Mount Greylock. You can visit all those places.

Herman wrote many books. Here is a list of the books he wrote. These were written before he moved to Arrowhead: *Typee*, *Omoo*, *Mardi* and *Redburn*. Here are the ones written while living at Arrowhead for the thirteen years he was there: *Moby Dick*, *White Jacket*, *Pierre*, *The Piazza Tales*, *I and My Chimney*, and *The Confidence Man*. After moving back to New York, Herman wrote a collection of poetry from his experience visiting the front lines of the Civil War; *Battle-Pieces and Aspects of War*. He also wrote *Clarel*, a 16,000-line epic poem that the critics bashed. In 1890, Herman gathered poems he had written as a gift for his wife, Lizzie. This collection is called *Weeds and Wildings, chiefly, With a Rose or Two*. In that collection is a story about Herman's favorite childhood tale, Rip Van Winkle as well as many lovely poems. And you all know his last book, *Billy Budd*.

Herman Melville died on September 28, 1891 at his home on 26th Street in New York City. Some newspapers reported that they thought he had been dead for twenty years. He was almost forgotten and had it not been for his granddaughter, Eleanor, we might never have known what a truly great writer he was. Because of her love for her grandfather, the world knows his name and his great works. He has not been forgotten. He lives on.

Herman Melville inspires me every day. Even though he only had a 6th grade education, he was a voracious reader and learned all he could by reading and experiencing life. And he wrote, no matter what. No matter whether his books were popular or not, he wrote. And he never gave up living a creative life. Even at the end of his life when he was a Customs Officer, working hard all day long at a job he didn't like, he continued to write. He wrote because he loved writing. And he wrote until the day he died. I think that's inspiring. I hope you do too.

Acknowledgments

I want to thank Betsy Sherman, former Director of the Berkshire Historical Society for inviting me to be Writer-In-Residence and for first telling me the story of Eleanor and the breadbox. Betsy's knowledge and love of Herman Melville is an inspiration to me. Thanks to Will Garrison, Curator and current Director of Arrowhead and the Berkshire Historical Society, for his wisdom, fact checking and insight into Herman Melville and the times in which he lived. Will's kind editorial comments helped to shape this book. Special thanks to Will's daughter Lucy for reading it over and over as it grew. If Lucy gave it a 'thumbs up', I knew I was on the right track. And thanks to Lucy and her sister Rose for choosing the best cover! Thanks to J. Peter Bergman, Arrowhead's Director of Communication and Community Relations, a poet, playwright and author whose wise suggestions, kind critiques, sense of humor and knowledge about my subject helped form my story. You three are the mainstay of my writing journey.

I want to thank Hershel Parker, whose books on Melville became my required reading. And thanks to Michael Shelden, whose new book and new insights gave me more of an understanding of Herman as a person. Thanks to Travis Daly for seeing the theatrical magic in my story and making Herman and Eleanor come to life on the stage!

Thank you to Dennis C. Marnon of the Houghton Library, Harvard University, Cambridge MA for permission to use the image of the letter from Herman to Bessie.

Thanks to my children, Sam and Zoë for listening to me go on for hours about Herman Melville and for encouraging me every step of the way. To my parents and sisters for always encouraging me to live my creative dreams. To Sean for his willingness to listen to me read and reread this story as it unfolded, and for loving it. And special thanks to my best friend, Nancy Tunnicliffe, for spotting the announcement about the residency and encouraging me to apply for it. It has changed my life in profound ways.

I want to thank Eleanor Melville Thomas Metcalf for allowing me to tell the story of her beloved grandfather through her voice. I hope I did her justice. And to Herman Melville, for guiding me from his unseen place, sitting next to me by his fairy window, and helping the words flow. I am so grateful.

Thank you.

Jana Laiz

Declan Kerr was born in Ireland, grew up in London and New York, and is still growing up, back in Ireland. He paints, illustrates and animates and has exhibited around Ireland and England. He says he can play guitar, but when he mentions this supposed talent his best buddy Alistair Bowie Kerr begs to disagree by scratching at the door to be let outside. Canine criticism of his musical talents aside, you can see more of Declan's work on his website, www.declan-kerr.com

Jana Laiz has been writing for as long as she can remember. She is the author of the triple Award Winning novel, *Weeping Under This Same Moon*, *The Twelfth Stone*, Book of the Year Award nominee and Kids' Indie Next List pick, *Elephants of the Tsunami*, written to raise money for tsunami relief, the co-author of "*A Free Woman On God's Earth, The True Story of Elizabeth "Mumbet" Freeman, The Slave Who Won Her Freedom*," soon to be a feature film, and *Simon Says: Tails Told By The Red Lion Inn Ambassador*. She is a teacher, a writer, an editor, a mom, an animal lover, a musician and a dreamer. She is passionate about our beautiful planet and endeavors to make a difference in the world. Jana is the very first Writer-in-Residence at Herman Melville's beloved Arrowhead. She lives in a 200-year-old farmhouse in the Berkshire Hills of Massachusetts. For book club and author visit information, visit www.janalaiz.com